154677   MG

JEREMY LIN

BY MARTY GITLIN

Published by ABDO Publishing Company, PO Box 398166, Minneapolis, MN 55439. Copyright © 2013 by Abdo Consulting Group, Inc. International copyrights reserved in all countries. No part of this book may be reproduced in any form without written permission from the publisher. SportsZone™ is a trademark and logo of ABDO Publishing Company.

Printed in the United States of America,
North Mankato, Minnesota
052012
092012

 THIS BOOK CONTAINS AT LEAST 10% RECYCLED MATERIALS.

Editor: Arnold Ringstad
Series Designer: Craig Hinton

Photo Credits: Jim Mone/AP Images, cover; Frank Gunn, The Canadian Press/AP Images, 4; Seth Poppel/Yearbook Library, 7; Frank Franklin II/AP Images, 8; Steve Yeater/AP Images, 10, 14; Paul Sakuma/AP Images, 13; Michael Dwyer/AP Images, 16; Elise Amendola/AP Images, 19; Lori Shepler/AP Images, 20; Wally Santana/AP Images, 23; Jim McIsaac/Getty Images, 25; Bill Kostroun/AP Images, 26; Chris Trotman/Getty Images, 28

Library of Congress Cataloging-in-Publication Data
Gitlin, Marty.
  Jeremy Lin : basketball phenom / Marty Gitlin.
     p. cm. -- (Playmakers)
  Includes index.
  ISBN 978-1-61783-548-3
  1. Lin, Jeremy, 1988---Juvenile literature. 2. Basketball players--United States--Biography--Juvenile literature. I. Title.
  GV884.L586G58 2013
  796.323092--dc23
  [B]
                          2012018276

TABLE OF CONTENTS

Jeremy Lin

CHAPTER 1

THE BIRTH OF "LINSANITY"

J eremy Lin held the basketball against his left hip. The new superstar of the New York Knicks glared at Toronto Raptors defender José Calderón.

The game was tied at 87–87 as the final seconds ticked away. The fans in Toronto chanted: "DEFENSE! DEFENSE! DEFENSE!" The Knicks needed a basket to claim their sixth straight victory. The Raptors needed a stop to send the game into overtime.

Jeremy Lin drives to the hoop against the Toronto Raptors in 2012.

It was February 14, 2012. Jeremy was the talk of the National Basketball Association (NBA). He had spent the entire game showing why. Jeremy had already scored 24 points. He also had 11 assists. Now he had a chance to hit the game-winning shot.

Jeremy inched forward. He was about 25 feet away from the basket. Calderón expected Jeremy to try to dribble around him. Instead, Jeremy leaped into the air and released a shot. The fans grew quiet as the ball flew toward the net. Then . . . *swish*! He made the basket, and the Knicks won the game.

Jeremy was an unlikely hero. His parents were both just 5-foot-6. Most NBA players have tall parents. His dad, Gie-Ming Lin, was a Taiwanese immigrant. Until Jeremy, no Taiwanese-

Jeremy's brothers also became fine basketball players. His older brother Joshua played in high school. He then pursued a career as a dentist. His younger brother Joseph plays on the Hamilton College team. Both brothers lived in New York when Jeremy began playing for the Knicks.

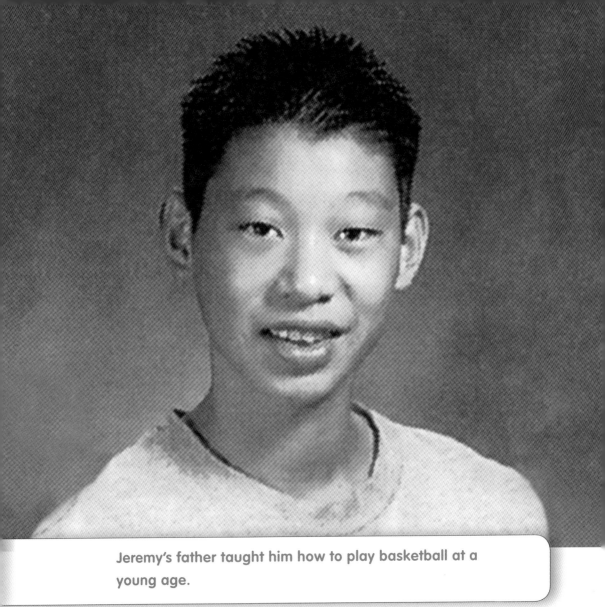

Jeremy's father taught him how to play basketball at a young age.

American had ever played in the NBA. And Jeremy had played college basketball at Harvard. Nobody from Harvard had played in the NBA for nearly 50 years.

In early 2012, "Linsanity" made products with Jeremy's name on them very popular.

The unlikely success story began before Jeremy's birth. Gie-Ming became interested in basketball while he was still living in Taiwan. He later moved to the United States to finish his education. Gie-Ming studied at Purdue University in Indiana. While there, he began watching basketball games on television.

The hype surrounding Jeremy's rise to fame became known as "Linsanity." "Linsanity" combines Jeremy's last name with the word "insanity." Some of Jeremy's former classmates tried to cash in on his fame. One middle school friend wanted to sell a yearbook signed by Lin for $4,800.

Gie-Ming became hooked on the sport. He taped games involving his favorite players. He tried to copy their moves. He decided he would someday show his future children how to play basketball.

Gie-Ming and his wife Shirley had three sons. Jeremy was the middle child. He was born in Los Angeles, California, on August 23, 1988. His father taught him the sport at a young age. Jeremy and his brothers would rush to do their homework. Then they would join Gie-Ming for basketball practice. That practice soon paid off.

Jeremy Lin

CHAPTER 2

ONWARD AND UPWARD

Jeremy was just 5-foot-3 as a freshman basketball player at Palo Alto High School. But he soon grew to 6-foot-3. He was a strong passer and a good shooter. He drove to the basket with skill and courage.

Jeremy's parents supported him every step of the way. Shirley would arrive an hour early for his games. She also would study the statistics of his opponents. But still, she was more concerned with Jeremy's

Jeremy drives to the hoop during the 2006 high school state championship game.

grades than his basketball success. Jeremy had a 4.2 grade-point average. That meant he got straight A's. He was also one of the best high school basketball players in the state. He could leap high enough to dunk the ball as a sophomore. His high school league named him the Most Valuable Player as a junior and senior. He showed all-around talent. Jeremy averaged 15.1 points, 7.1 assists, 5.0 steals, and 6.2 rebounds per game as a senior. Jeremy even led his team to a state title that season.

But along the way he was forced to overcome prejudice. It was rare for a Taiwanese-American to be a basketball standout. Some fans were not accepting of it. They screamed from the stands that he belonged in the orchestra or on the math team. Others called out racial slurs to him during games.

Jeremy's father taught him to perform on the court. He also taught Jeremy how to deal with the taunts. Gie-Ming told

Jeremy finished his high school career strong. He led Palo Alto High School to a 32–1 record as a senior. Powerful Mater Dei was then favored over Palo Alto in the state championship game. Instead, Jeremy led his school to a 51–47 upset victory.

Jeremy's parents Shirley and Gie-Ming supported his dream of playing basketball.

Jeremy people would respect him if he helped his team win basketball games.

Jeremy did help his team win games. Still, not everyone accepted him. Jeremy had led his high school team to a state

Jeremy Lin

title. But he did not catch the attention of many Division I college basketball programs. Division I is the highest level of college sports.

The University of California, Los Angeles (UCLA) was a basketball powerhouse. A scout from the school watched Jeremy in the state championship game. UCLA offered Jeremy a chance to try out for the team. But they did not offer him a scholarship. Neither did other schools. Jeremy would have to make it some other way. And he did just that.

Jeremy celebrates with teammates after winning a 2006 California high school state championship.

Jeremy Lin

CHAPTER 3

THE COLLEGE YEARS

It was a summer afternoon in July 2005. Jeremy Lin was trying to show off his talent to college coaches in a Las Vegas gym. But he was not playing well.

Harvard assistant coach Bill Holden watched Lin play. He was not impressed. He told Lin's high school coach that Harvard was not interested in recruiting Lin. Holden said Lin belonged in a smaller Division III basketball program.

DISCARD

Lin protects the ball during Harvard's 2007 game against Michigan.

But Holden was lucky. He got a chance to watch Lin again a week later. Lin played better and with more intensity. Holden was now convinced to recruit Lin. Harvard is one of the top schools in the country. And it is in Massachusetts. That is far from Lin's home in Palo Alto. But it gave him a chance to play Division I basketball. Soon, he was traveling to the East Coast.

In his first year at Harvard, Lin averaged nearly five points and two assists per game. He became a full-time starter as a sophomore. But his dream of an NBA career still seemed far away. During seven games in early 2008, he made just 23 of 69 shots. Harvard ended the season with a terrible 8–22 record.

Lin improved the following year. He scored at least 10 points in almost every game. Harvard finished with a 14–14 record. Lin became even better as a senior. In one game against the Connecticut Huskies, he exploded for 30 points and nine

Some believe Jeremy's race played a role in him being ignored by college basketball scouts. They might have thought an Asian American could not succeed in basketball. A 2009 study found that only 20 of the 5,051 Division I players were Asian Americans.

Lin scrambles for the ball during a 2009 game against Boston College.

rebounds. On the season, he averaged 16.4 points per game and posted career highs in assists and steals. He also showed deadly accuracy by hitting 52 percent of his shots.

But just as college programs ignored him four years earlier, professional teams ignored him in the 2010 NBA Draft. Lin would have to find another path to make his dream a reality.

20 Jeremy Lin

CHAPTER 4

TAKING THE WORLD BY STORM

Jeremy Lin's road to stardom began on the Dallas Mavericks' summer team. NBA teams use these teams to help young players develop and to try to identify hidden gems. Lin averaged just 19 minutes of playing time in the first five games. Time was running out for him to show he belonged.

The Mavericks' last summer game was against the Washington Wizards. Lin stole the show. He made

Lin goes for a layup in a 2010 game against the Los Angeles Lakers.

a steal, ripped away a rebound, drove in for a layup, and nailed a three-pointer. His performance created interest from NBA teams. The Golden State Warriors offered Lin a contract. His hard work was finally rewarded.

Interest from NBA fans began right away. Lin played his first game in the preseason. The fans chanted for him as he sat on the bench in the third quarter. When he finally checked into the game, he received huge applause. Fans cheered every time Lin touched the ball. He was moved by the cheers.

Lin was soon familiar with "garbage time." This means time played when one team was clearly going to win. The Warriors lost 11 straight games with Lin playing. He missed 10 of his first 12 shots that season. He later hit a slump in which he missed 14 of 16.

Lin was sent down to the NBA Development League several times. This is a lower league where players can improve their skills. Each time he showed he belonged in the NBA. He was sent to play in Reno twice by Golden State. He responded by averaging 18 points per game.

After signing with the Golden State Warriors, Lin became very popular in Taiwan.

The Warriors cut Lin before the 2011–12 season. The Houston Rockets signed him, but he was cut again on Christmas Eve in 2011.

The disappointment soon turned into joy. The New York Knicks signed Lin. He hoped to impress Knicks coach Mike D'Antoni. Lin still received attention for being an Asian-American player. He set out to prove he was a talented player who belonged in the NBA. Lin appeared in only nine of the Knicks' first 23 games. He played for more than seven minutes in only one game.

Lin was earning the lowest salary possible for an NBA player. He knew he could again be cut from the team soon. He was sleeping on the couch in his brother Joshua's home. Joshua was a dental student at New York University. When Joshua had a guest who needed the couch, Lin slept on the couch of his Knicks teammate Landry Fields. Lin even talked about quitting basketball.

He didn't know that he would soon be one of the biggest sports stars in the world. When D'Antoni became tired of poor performance from his guards, he decided to give Lin more playing time.

The Golden State Warriors are located in the Bay Area of California. This area includes the cities of San Francisco and Oakland. The region is home to a large Asian-American population. There was much excitement for Lin's arrival. His website received 20,000 views on the day he signed.

Lin took the New York Knicks and the world by storm in February 2012.

Lin finally had a chance to prove himself in early February 2012. He recorded 25 points and seven assists against the New Jersey Nets. He then scored 28 points with eight assists against Utah. And he added 23 points and 10 assists against Washington. New York won all three games.

"Linsanity" had begun. The fans cheered louder for Lin than for any of his teammates. They waived Taiwanese flags and chanted his name.

Lin drives to the basket during a February 2012 game against the New Jersey Nets.

Nobody could have predicted how much better it would get. The Los Angeles Lakers were the next opponents on the schedule for the Knicks. Before the game, Lakers superstar

The success of an Asian American in the NBA sparked great interest in China. Lin's account on Weibo (that country's version of Twitter) had a few hundred followers in January 2012. By late February, it had more than a million.

Kobe Bryant was asked about "Linsanity." He claimed he had never heard of it.

Bryant and the Lakers learned about it quickly. Lin hit a three-pointer two minutes into the game. One minute later, he hit a jump shot. Two minutes later, he hit another jump shot. Fifteen seconds later, he scored on a layup. Two minutes later, he hit two foul shots. Lin finished with a stunning 38 points in a 92–85 victory.

The Rockets had cut Lin just two months earlier. Now he was a worldwide sensation. The Knicks ran off seven straight wins before losing to the New Orleans Hornets. The defending NBA champion Dallas Mavericks were next on the Knicks' schedule. Some believed the Mavericks would shut down Lin. Instead, he scored 28 points. Lin also added 14 assists and five steals in another win.

Lin and the crowd react after he hits a three-pointer against the Dallas Mavericks.

Lin averaged an amazing 23.9 points, 9.2 assists, and 2.4 steals in 11 games. He led the Knicks to a 9–2 record. He also hit 50 percent of his shots. Lin's popularity had exploded. His No. 17 jersey was the top seller in the NBA. And sales on the team's online store went up by 4,000 percent.

Even President Barack Obama took notice of "Linsanity." He praised Lin to staff members after watching him defeat Toronto with a game-winning three-pointer.

The "Linsanity" cooled off a bit after that. The Knicks lost six games in a row in March 2012. Coach Mike D'Antoni was fired later that month. Finally, in late March, Lin suffered a season-ending knee injury. He had surgery on his knee in April, and missed the rest of the 2011–12 regular season. But nobody could question the impact Jeremy Lin had already made on the Knicks and the NBA.

FUN FACTS AND QUOTES

- The publicity surrounding "Linsanity" resulted in rumors about Lin. One rumor claimed that Lin was dating reality TV star and model Kim Kardashian. Lin said in a television interview that the rumor was untrue.

- Lin was thrilled after signing his first NBA contract. "I just remember saying, 'I can't believe this!'" he recalled about signing with Golden State. "I was yelling. I was fist-pumping. I was screaming. I can't remember all that I said, but if you were anywhere near my house, you probably would have heard me."

- Ice cream company Ben & Jerry's noticed Lin's popularity. They created a frozen yogurt flavor called "Taste the Lin-Sanity." But some people were upset because the flavor included fortune cookies. They were offended because the fortune cookies were seen as a reference to his Chinese ethnicity. Ben & Jerry's later apologized and replaced the fortune cookies with waffle cones.

- Lin was recognized for his talent at Harvard. He was a finalist for the Bob Cousy Award, which is presented to the top college point guard in the country. Lin did not win. The honor went to Greivis Vasquez of the University of Maryland.

WEB LINKS

To learn more about Jeremy Lin, visit ABDO Publishing Company online at **www.abdopublishing.com**. Websites about Lin are featured on our Book Links page. These links are routinely monitored and updated to provide the most current information available.

GLOSSARY

assist
A pass that directly results in a scored basket.

draft
An annual event in which the top amateur basketball players are selected by NBA teams.

immigrant
A person who moves to another country.

layup
A short shot at the basket, often banked off the backboard.

overtime
An extra session of basketball if the game remains tied after regulation play.

point guard
A position on a basketball team greatly responsible for handling and passing the ball.

prejudice
A dislike of someone or something for no reason, sometimes based on race.

rebound
To catch the ball after a missed shot.

recruit
A high school or college player being sought to play at the next level.

scholarship
Financial assistance awarded to students to help them pay for school. Top athletes earn scholarships to represent a college through its sports teams.

three-pointer
A made shot from a long distance that counts for three points instead of two.

INDEX

FURTHER RESOURCES

Dalrymple, Timothy. *Jeremy Lin: The Reason for the Linsanity*. New York: Center Street, 2012.

Knobel, Andy. *New York Knicks*. Edina, MN: ABDO Publishing Co., 2012.

Yorkey, Mike. *Linspired: The Remarkable Rise of Jeremy Lin*. Grand Rapids, MI: Zondervan, 2012.